Nicholas
Again

RENÉ GOSCINNY & JEAN-JACQUES SEMPÉ

Translated by Anthea Bell

Φ

Phaidon Press Inc
180 Varick Street
New York, NY 10014

www.phaidon.com

This edition © 2006 Phaidon Press Limited
First published in French as *Les récrés du petit Nicolas*
by Éditions Denoël © 1961 Éditions Denoël
New French edition © 2002 Éditions Denoël

ISBN 0 7148 4564 7 (US edition)

A CIP catalogue record for this book is available
from the British Library.

Designed by Chiara Bianchini, James Cartledge,
and Phil Cleaver of etal-design.

Printed in China

CONTENTS

Uncle George's Nose

Dad walked to school with me after lunch today. I like it when Dad goes with me, because he often gives me money to buy things, and that's what he did today. We were passing the toyshop, and I looked in the window and saw those cardboard noses you can put on your face to make your friends laugh.

"Oh, Dad, do buy me a nose!" I said. Dad said no, he wouldn't, I didn't need a nose, but I showed him a red one and I said, "Oh, please, Dad! Buy me that nose, it's just like Uncle George's!"

Uncle George is Dad's brother; he's fat and he tells a lot of stories, and he's always laughing. We don't see him very often because he travels around selling things in faraway places, Lyon and Marseille and Bordeaux. Dad started to laugh.

"You're right," said Dad, "it is like a smaller version of George's nose! I'll put it on next time he comes to see us!"

And then we went into the shop and bought the nose, and I put it on. It had an elastic band to keep it in place. Then Dad put it on, and then the lady in the shop put it back on me, and we all looked at ourselves in the mirror and laughed a lot. I don't care what anyone says, my Dad is great!

When he left me at the school gates, Dad said, "Now, be good; try not to make any trouble with George's nose." I promised and I went into school.

I saw our gang in the playground, and I put on my nose to show them and we all laughed a lot.

"It's like my Auntie Claire's nose," said Max.

"No, it's my Uncle George's nose," I said. "You remember – my uncle the explorer."

"Lend me that nose, will you?" Eddie asked.

"No!" I said. "Ask your own Dad to buy one if you want one!"

"If you don't lend it, I'm going to punch it!" said Eddie, who is very strong, and biff! he punched Uncle George's nose.

It didn't hurt, but I was afraid Eddie might have broken Uncle George's nose, so I put it in my pocket and I kicked him. We were in the middle of fighting and the rest of the gang were watching, when Old Spuds came chasing up. Old Spuds is one of the teachers, and some day I'll tell you why we call him Spuds.

"What's going on here?" asked Old Spuds.

"It's Eddie!" I said. "He punched my nose and he broke it!"

Old Spuds seemed very surprised, and he bent down with his face right next to mine, and he said, "Let's have a look ..."

So I took Uncle George's nose out of my pocket and showed him. I don't know why, but the sight of Uncle George's nose made him very angry.

"Boy, look me in the eye!" said Old Spuds, standing up again. "I don't stand for people making fun of me, my young friend! You'll stay in after school today, understand?"

I started to cry, and Geoffrey said, "Please, sir, it wasn't his fault, sir."

Old Spuds looked at Geoffrey and smiled and patted his shoulder.

"Confessing to save a friend, eh? Well done, my boy!"

"Well, it wasn't his fault," said Geoffrey, "it was Eddie's fault."

Old Spuds went bright red. He opened and shut his mouth several times before he said anything, and then he gave Eddie detention and he gave Geoffrey detention and he gave Matthew detention for laughing. And he went off to ring the bell.

Back in the classroom, our teacher began telling us things about when France was full of Gauls. Alec, who was sitting next to me, asked if Uncle George's nose was really broken. I said no, just a bit squashed at the end, and I took it out of my pocket to see if I could put it right. And when I pushed my finger inside it, I managed to get it back into the same shape it was before, so I was very pleased.

"Put it on, to make sure," said Alec.

So I bent down under my desk and put the nose on. Alec took a look and said, "That's OK, it's fine."

"Nicholas! Tell me what I have been saying," said our teacher suddenly. She gave me a nasty fright.

I sat up very suddenly, and I felt like crying, because I hadn't the faintest idea what our teacher had just been saying and she doesn't like people not listening to her. Our teacher stared at me, very surprised, like Old Spuds.

"What on earth have you got on your face?" she asked me.

"It's the nose Dad bought me," I explained, crying.

Our teacher was cross, and she started to shout and say she disliked clowns, and if I carried on like this I should get expelled from school and finish up an ignoramus and be a disgrace to my parents, and then she said, "Bring me that nose!"

So I went and put it on her desk, still crying, and she said she was confiscating it, and then she told me to write fifty lines saying, "I must not bring cardboard noses into History with the aim of playing the fool and making my friends misbehave."

When I got home, Mom looked at me and she said, "Whatever is the matter with you, Nicholas? You do look pale!" So I started to cry, and I told her how Old Spuds had given me detention when I took Uncle George's nose out of my pocket, and how our teacher had given me fifty lines to write because of Uncle George's nose, and then she had gone and confiscated it. Mom looked very startled, and then she put a hand on my forehead and said I'd better go and lie down for a while and rest.

When Dad came home from the office, Mom told him, "I've been so worried, I could hardly wait for you to get home!

8

Nicholas came back from school in a very odd, nervous condition. I wonder if I ought to call the doctor for him?"

"I might have known it!" said Dad. "And I did warn him, too! I bet that little wretch has been fooling around with old George's nose!"

And then we were all very worried, because Mom felt ill and we had to call the doctor for her.

Alec is Expelled

Something really awful happened at school today: Alec was expelled! It all started at second recess in the morning.

We were playing dodgeball. I expect you know the rules: the one with the ball is It, and he throws the ball and tries to hit someone else, and then the other person cries, and then it's his turn to be It. Dodgeball is a great game. The only ones not playing were Geoffrey, who was absent that day, Cuthbert, who always does revision during break, and Alec, who was eating his last jam sandwich of the morning. Alec always keeps his biggest sandwich for second recess, which is slightly longer than the other recess periods. Eddie was It, which is unusual; he's so strong that we always try not to hit him with the ball, because when he's It and he throws the ball back, it hurts a lot. Well, Eddie aimed at Matthew, who flung himself on the ground, covering his head with his hands, and the ball passed right over him, and wham! it hit Alec right in the middle of his back, and he dropped the jam sandwich and it came apart and fell jam side down. Alec was not at all pleased; he went scarlet in the face and started yelling, and Old Spuds, who is one of the teachers, came running up to see what was going on. What he didn't see, though, was the jam sandwich, and he slipped on it and nearly fell over. Old Spuds was very surprised,

11

and he got jam all over his shoe. Alec was in a terrible state, waving his arms around and shouting, "What a daft thing to do! Honestly, can't you look where you're going, you clumsy great oaf?"

In fact, Alec was absolutely furious. The thing is you must never, never mess around with Alec's things to eat, specially not his big jam sandwich at second recess. Old Spuds wasn't in the best of tempers, either.

"Boy, look me in the eye!" he said. "Now, what was that you said?"

"I said you've got no right to go trampling all over my sandwiches, you clumsy great oaf!" said Alec.

So Old Spuds took Alec by the arm and led him away. He went squelch! squelch! as he walked, because of the jam on his shoe.

And then Mr. Morrison rang the bell for the end of recess. Mr. Morrison is a new teacher and we haven't had time to think up a name for him yet. We went into our classroom, and Alec still wasn't back. Our teacher was surprised.

"Where can Alec be?" she asked.

We were just going to tell her when the classroom door opened and in came the Principal, with Alec and Old Spuds.

"Stand up, boys!" said our teacher.

"Sit down, boys!" said the Principal.

The Principal was not looking pleased. Nor was Old Spuds, and as for Alec, his face was red with crying, and he was sniffling.

"Now, boys," said the Principal, "your little friend here has been extremely rude to Old Sp – to Mr. Goodman. I can find no excuse whatever for such lack of respect toward an older person in a position of authority! Therefore, your little friend is being expelled from school. Of course, he didn't think of the suffering he would cause his parents, oh, no! If he doesn't mend his ways in future he'll end up in jail, which, let me tell you, is the fate of all ignoramuses. And I hope this will be a lesson to you all!"

So then the Principal told Alec to collect his things. Alec collected them, crying, and then he went off with the Principal and Old Spuds.

We were all very sad, including our teacher. "I'll see what I can do about it," she promised us.

I must say, our teacher is sometimes really great.

When we came out of school, we saw Alec waiting for us at the corner, eating a little chocolate croissant. When we got close to him, we saw how sad he was looking.

"Haven't you been home yet?" I asked.

"No," said Alec, "but I'll have to now because it's lunchtime, and when I tell Mom and Dad, I bet they won't let me have any dessert! What a day!"

So off went Alec, dragging his feet and munching very slowly. We got the impression that he almost had to force himself to eat. Poor old Alec, we were ever so upset.

But a little later, when we were back in our classroom, the Principal came in with Alec, who was smiling all over his face.

"Stand up, boys!" said our teacher.

"Sit down, boys!" said the Principal.

And then he told us he'd decided to give Alec another chance. He said that he did so out of consideration for our little friend's parents, who hated to think of their son running the risk of jail because of being an ignoramus.

"Your little friend has apologized to Mr. Goodman, who has

been kind enough to accept his apologies," said the Principal. "And I hope that your friend will be grateful for his generosity and that, having learnt his lesson, he will take warning from it. I am sure that he will make up for the serious offence he committed today by his future behavior. That's right, isn't it?"

"Er ... yes," said Alec.

The Principal looked at him, opened his mouth, sighed, and left the room.

We were very pleased. We all started talking at once, but our teacher tapped the desk with her ruler and said, "Sit down, everyone! Alec, go back to your place and behave yourself. Matthew, come up to the blackboard."

When the bell went for recess we all went down to the playground, except for Matthew who had detention, which he gets every time he is asked any questions. Out in the playground, while Alec was eating his cheese sandwich, we asked him what had happened in the Principal's office, and then Old Spuds came along.

"Come on, now!" he said, "leave your little friend alone. This morning's incident is closed, so run along and play!"

And he took hold of Max's arm, and Max jostled Alec, and Alec dropped his cheese sandwich.

Alec looked at Old Spuds and went bright scarlet in the face and started waving his arms around.

"There you go again!" he shouted. "This really is the end! Honestly, will you never learn, you clumsy great oaf?"

My Watch

When I got back from school yesterday afternoon, the mailman had brought a parcel for me. It was a present from Granny.

A fantastic present! You'll never guess what it was – a watch! My Granny is really great, and so is my watch, and the rest of the gang will be terribly impressed. Dad wasn't at home because he had a business dinner that evening, but Mom showed me how to wind the watch and she put it on my wrist. Luckily, I'm very good at telling the time, not like last year when I was little and I'd have had to go around asking people what my watch said all the time, which would have been a bit tricky. The really good thing about my watch was the big hand which went round much faster than the other two; you can't see them move at all unless you look very hard for a very long time. I asked Mom what the big hand was for, and she said it was very useful for telling you when boiled eggs were done.

It was a pity there weren't any boiled eggs when Mom and I sat down to our supper at 7.32 p.m. I kept looking at my watch while I ate, and Mom told me to hurry up or my soup would get cold, so I finished my soup in exactly the time it took the biggest hand to go round twice and a bit. At 7.51 p.m. Mom brought in the end of the yummy dessert left over from lunchtime, and we finished supper at 7.58 p.m. Mom let me play for a bit. I held the watch to my ear to hear it tick, and at 8.15 p.m. Mom told me to go to bed. I felt as happy as I did that time I was given the fountain pen which made blots everywhere! I wanted to keep my watch on when I went to sleep, but Mom told me it wouldn't be good for it, so I put it on my bedside table where I could see it quite easily if I turned over on my side, and Mom put the light out at 8.38 p.m.

Then it was fantastic, because the numbers and the hands of my watch shone in the dark! I wouldn't have needed to put the light on even if I'd wanted to boil some eggs. I didn't feel like going to sleep. I kept looking at my watch all the time, so I heard when the front door opened. It was Dad coming home. I was very pleased, because now I could show him Granny's present. I got up and put on my watch and went out of my bedroom.

I saw Dad coming upstairs on tiptoe. "Hey, Dad!" I shouted. "Look at the lovely watch Granny gave me!" Dad was very startled, so startled he nearly fell downstairs. "Ssh, Nicholas!" he said. "Ssh, you'll wake your mother up!" And the light went

on and we saw Mom coming out of her bedroom. "His mother is already awake," said Mom to Dad, not looking very pleased, and then she asked if this was any time to get home from a business dinner. "Oh, really!" said Dad. "It's not all that late."

"It's exactly 11.58 p.m.," I said. I felt very proud of myself, because I do like being helpful to Mom and Dad.

"Wonderful presents your mother thinks up, I must say!" Dad told Mom.

"This is a fine time to discuss my mother!" said Mom. "Especially in front of Nicholas!" She didn't look as if she was standing for any nonsense. Then she told me to go back to bed, darling, and have a nice sleep.

I went back to my room and I heard Dad and Mom talking for a bit, and I started my nice sleep at 12.14 a.m.

I woke up at 5.07 a.m.; it was beginning to get light, which was a pity, because the numbers on my watch didn't shine so brightly then. I was in no hurry to get up because there wasn't any school today, but I told myself I might be able to be helpful to Dad again; he's always complaining that his boss is always complaining that he's late at the office. So I waited a bit and at 5.12 a.m. I went into Mom and Dad's room and I shouted, "It's morning, Dad! You'll be late for the office!" Dad looked very startled, but it wasn't as dangerous as when he was startled on the stairs, because he couldn't fall downstairs when he was in bed. All the same, Dad did look funny, as if he had fallen downstairs. Mom woke up too, with a jump. "What is it? What's the matter?" she asked.

"It's that watch of his," said Dad. "Apparently, it's morning."

"That's right," I said. "It's 5.15 a.m. Soon it will be 5.16 a.m."

"Well done, Nicholas," said Mom, "and now go back to bed – we're awake, all right."

I went back to bed, but I had to go back to Mom and Dad three times, at 5.47 a.m., 6.18 a.m. and 7.02 a.m., before they finally got up.

We were sitting down to breakfast and Dad called Mom, "Hurry up with the coffee, dear, or I shall be late. I've been waiting five minutes now."

"Eight," I said, and Mom came in and she looked at me in a funny sort of way. When she poured out the coffee she spilt some on the tablecloth because her hand was trembling. Poor Mom, I do hope she isn't sick.

"I'll be home in good time for lunch," said Dad. "Expect to see me clocking in at the door." I asked Mom what clocking in meant, but she told me to take no notice and go and play outside.

It's the first time I was ever sorry there was no school, because I wanted to show the gang my watch. The only other person who once came to school with a watch was Geoffrey, who brought his Dad's watch, a big fat one with a lid and a chain. Geoffrey's Dad's watch was great, but it turned out that Geoffrey wasn't supposed to take it and there was a lot of trouble and we never saw that watch again, and Geoffrey told us he got such a thrashing that we jolly nearly never saw him again, either.

I went off to see Alec, my fat friend who lives near me and eats a lot. I know Alec gets up early because it takes him so long to have breakfast. "Hi, Alec!" I called when I got to his house. "Alec! Come and see what I've got!" Alec came out with a croissant in his hand and another in his mouth. "Look, it's a watch!" I told Alec, raising my arm to the level of the end of the croissant which was in his mouth. Alec squinted at it and swallowed and said, "That's not bad!"

"It goes ever so well and it has a hand for boiling eggs and it shines in the dark," I told him.

"What does it look like inside?" Alec asked.

I hadn't thought of looking inside. "Wait a minute," said Alec, and he went back into his house and came out again with another croissant and a penknife. "Give me your watch," said Alec. "I'll open it up with my knife. I know how, I've already opened my Dad's watch." So I gave Alec my watch and he got to work on it with his penknife. Then I was afraid he might break my watch, and I said to him, "Give me my watch back!" But Alec didn't want to, he put out his tongue and went on trying to open the watch. So then I tried to get it back from him by force, and the penknife slipped and cut Alec's finger, and Alec yelped, and the watch came open and it dropped on the ground at 9.10 a.m. It was still 9.10 a.m. when I got home, crying. My watch didn't work anymore. Mom hugged me and told me Dad would fix it.

When Dad came home for lunch, Mom gave him my watch. Dad turned the little knob and looked at Mom and looked at the watch and looked at me, and then he said, "Listen, Nicholas, this watch can't be mended. But that doesn't mean you can't have fun with it, not in the least! You don't have to worry about breaking it now, and it will look just as good as ever on your wrist." And he looked so pleased and Mom looked so pleased that I was pleased, too.

So now my watch always says four o'clock, which is a nice time, because four o'clock is teatime and we have little chocolate croissants. And the numbers still shine in the dark.

Granny's present is fantastic!

Our Newspaper

At break, Max showed us the present his godmother had given him: it was a printing set. It's a box with lots of little rubber letters in it, and you put the letters into a frame and make any word you want. Then you press it down on a pad full of ink like in the post office, and then on a piece of paper, and there are the words, all printed like the newspaper Dad reads and he gets cross because Mom has taken the pages with clothes and special offers and recipes out. Max's printing set is terrific!

Max showed us what he'd already done with it. He took three pieces of paper out of his pocket; they had "Max" printed on them lots and lots of times, in all different directions.

"It's much better than when I write my name with a pen," said Max. He was right, too.

"Listen, everyone!" said Rufus. "Why don't we start a newspaper?"

That was a really fantastic idea, and we all agreed, even Cuthbert, who is teacher's pet and doesn't usually play with us at recess, he does revision instead. Cuthbert is nuts!

"What shall we call our paper?" I asked.

We couldn't agree about that. Some people wanted to call it *The Superb* and some wanted to call it *The Victor* or *The Fantastic* or *The Fearless*. Max wanted to call it *The Max*, and he

got annoyed when Alec said that was a stupid name and personally he'd rather the paper was called *The Gourmet*, which is the name of the delicatessen near his house. So we decided to settle the name later.

"What do we put in this paper, then?" asked Matthew.

"The same kind of thing they put in real newspapers," said Geoffrey. "Lots of news and photographs and drawings, and stories all about robberies and murders, and the stock exchange prices."

We didn't know what stock exchange prices were, so Geoffrey explained that they were lots of numbers in tiny little print, and his Dad was more interested in them than anything else in the paper. But you can't believe everything Geoffrey says; he's an awful liar, he'll try anything on.

"I can't print photographs," said Max. "I've only got letters in my printing set."

"But we can do drawings," I said. "I can draw a castle with people attacking it, and airships, and planes dropping bombs."

"I can draw a map of France showing all the different regions," said Cuthbert.

"I once did a drawing of my Mom putting her rollers in," said Matthew, "only my Mom tore it up. Dad laughed a lot when he saw it, though."

"That's all very well," said Max, "but if you fill up the paper with your scruffy old drawings there won't be any room left to print the really interesting things."

I asked Max if he wanted to be thumped, but Jeremy said Max was right, and he, Jeremy, had written a composition about Spring and he got seven out of ten for it, and it would look great in print, it was all about the pretty flowers and the birds going tweet-tweet.

"You don't really think we're going to use Max's letters to print your soppy birds going tweet-tweet, do you?" asked Rufus, and there was a fight.

"I could set sums, and we'd ask people to send us in the answers," said Cuthbert. "And we'd give them marks."

That made us laugh a lot. So Cuthbert started to cry. He said we were all very naughty, and we were always laughing at him, and he was going to complain to our teacher, and we'd all get punished, and he wasn't going to say another word, and it would jolly well serve us right.

What with Jeremy and Rufus fighting and Cuthbert crying, we could hardly hear ourselves speak. It isn't easy, running a newspaper with your friends!

"What do we do with the paper once it's printed?" asked Eddie.

"Talk about daft questions!" said Max. "Sell it, of course! That's what papers are for; you sell them and you get rich and you can buy yourself lots of things."

"Who do you sell them to?" I asked.

"Er, well … people," said Alec. "In the street. You run up and down shouting, 'Late Extra!' and everyone gives you their money."

"But there'll only be one newspaper," said Matthew, "so we won't get much money."

"Well, I'll tell the person I sell it to that it's very expensive," said Alec.

"Why you? I'm going to sell it," said Matthew. "You've always got sticky fingers, for one thing, so you'd make marks on our paper and no one would want to buy it."

"I'll show you whether I've got sticky fingers!" said Alec, and he planted them right in Matthew's face, and I was surprised because usually Alec doesn't like to fight at recess, it stops him eating. But Alec was really feeling very annoyed, and Rufus and Jeremy moved up a bit to make room for him and Matthew to fight. It was true, though, Alec does have sticky fingers. When you shake hands with him, they kind of cling to yours.

"Right, so we're all agreed: I'm editor of the paper," said Max.

"Oh, are we? Why you?" asked Eddie.

"Because it's my printing set, that's why," said Max.

"Wait a minute!" shouted Rufus. "I got the idea of the newspaper, so I'm the editor!"

"Hey, come back, you!" said Jeremy. "We're in the middle of our fight!"

"Well, you got what was coming to you, didn't you?" said Rufus, whose nose was bleeding.

"Don't make me laugh!" said Jeremy, who was covered in scratches, and they went back to fighting, next to Alec and Matthew.

"Say that again about sticky fingers!" shouted Alec.

"Sticky fingers! Sticky fingers!" shouted Matthew.

"I'm the editor, Max," said Eddie, "and you'd better admit it if you don't want a punch on the nose!"

"You think I'm scared of you?" asked Max, and personally, I think he was, because while he said it he was taking little steps backward, so then Eddie pushed Max, and he dropped the printing set and the little letters went all over the place. Max went red in the face and flung himself on Eddie. I tried to pick the letters up, but Max trod on my hand, so when Eddie had made a bit of room for me I hit Max, and then Old Spuds, who is one of the teachers but that isn't his real name, came to separate us. And that wasn't much fun, because he confiscated the printing set, he told us we were all a disgrace, he gave us detention, he went to ring the bell, and he took Cuthbert, who was feeling ill, off to the sickroom. One way and another, Old Spuds was kept pretty busy. So we won't be printing any newspaper after all. Old Spuds isn't going to give back the printing set till the summer vacation.

Anyway, there wouldn't have been anything to put in the paper. Nothing ever happens to us.

The Pink Vase

I was at home, playing with my ball, when crash! I broke the pink vase in the living room.

Mom came running in and I started to cry.

"Oh, Nicholas!" said Mom. "You know you're not allowed to play soccer indoors! Now look what you've done – you've gone and broken the pink vase! Your father loved that vase. When he comes home you must tell him what you've done and he'll punish you, and I hope it will be a lesson to you!"

Mom picked up the broken pieces of vase from the carpet, and she went back to the kitchen. I went on crying, because I knew there'd be trouble with Dad over the vase.

Dad came home from the office, and he sat down in his armchair and opened his paper and started to read. Mom called me into the kitchen and said, "Well, have you told Daddy what you did yet?"

"I don't want to tell him," I told her, and I cried a lot more.

"Oh, Nicholas, you know I don't like this sort of thing!" said Mom. "You must learn to be brave; you're a big boy now! Off you go to the living room and confess to Daddy."

I'll tell you something: every time anyone tells me I'm a big boy now it means trouble ahead. But Mum looked as if she meant it, so I went back to the living room.

"Dad ..." I said.

"Mmph?" said Dad, still reading the paper.

"I broke the pink vase," I said very quickly. There was a big lump in my throat.

"Mmph?" said Dad. "Very good, dear, run along and play."

I went back to the kitchen feeling ever so pleased, and Mom asked, "Well, did you tell Daddy?"

"Yes," I said.

"And what did he say?" asked Mom.

"He said it was very good, dear, and to run along and play," I said.

Mom didn't seem pleased. "Really!" she said, and she marched off to the living room.

"Well, I must say!" said Mom. "Is this the way you bring up your son?"

Dad looked up from his paper. He seemed very surprised.

"What was that?" he asked.

"Oh, you needn't pretend to me!" said Mom. "I can see you'd prefer to be left to read your paper in peace while I have to maintain discipline!"

"You're right there!" said Dad. "I would prefer to be left to read my paper in peace, but evidently that's too much to ask in this house!"

"Oh, yes, my lord likes to take it easy! Sitting reading the paper with his slippers on, while I do all the dirty work!" shouted Mom. "And then I suppose you'll be surprised if your son goes off the rails."

"Look, what on earth do you expect me to do?" shouted Dad. "Give the boy a thrashing the moment I get into the house?"

"You're ignoring your responsibilities, that's what!" said

Mom. "You hardly take any interest in your family at all!"

"Oh, for goodness' sake!" said Dad. "I work like crazy, I put up with my boss's bad moods, I make all sorts of sacrifices to provide you and Nicholas with all that ..."

"I've already told you not to discuss money in front of Nicholas!" said Mom.

"Really, you'll drive me crazy!" said Dad. "But we're not going on like this, oh no, indeed we are not!"

"My mother always warned me!" said Mom. "I ought to have listened to her."

"Oh, yes, your mother! I was wondering why your mother hadn't been dragged into this conversation earlier," said Dad.

"You leave my mother out of this!" said Mom. "I forbid you to mention my mother!"

"But it wasn't me who ..." Dad began, and the doorbell rang.

It was our next-door neighbor, Mr. Billings.

"Just dropped in to see if you'd like a game of checkers," he said to Dad.

"You couldn't have come at a better moment, Mr. Billings," said Mom. "You can give us an unbiased opinion. Don't you think a father ought to take an active part in the upbringing of his son?"

"What do you suppose he knows about it?" asked Dad. "He hasn't got any children."

"That makes no difference!" said Mom. "Dentists never have toothache, but that doesn't stop them being dentists!"

"Wherever did you get the notion that dentists never have toothache?"

asked Dad. "Honestly, you make me laugh!" And he laughed.

"You see, Mr. Billings? He just sits there laughing at me," cried Mom. "He makes stupid jokes instead of attending to his own son! Well, what do you think, Mr. Billings?"

"I think you haven't got time for a game of checkers just now," said Mr. Billings, "so I'll be off!"

"Oh no, you don't!" said Mom. "You wanted to shove your oar into this conversation, so you can just stay till it's finished!"

"No, he can't, the old fool!" said Dad. "Nobody asked him to come! He can just go back to his hovel!"

"Wait a moment ..." said Mr. Billings.

"You men, you're all the same!" said Mom. "Backing each other up! Why don't you go home, Mr. Billings, instead of listening at other people's doors?"

"Well, we'll have a game of checkers some other day," said Mr. Billings. "Goodbye, then! So long, Nicholas."

And Mr. Billings left.

I don't like it when Mom and Dad have an argument, but I do like it when they make up again, and sure enough, they soon made up their quarrel this time. Mom started to cry, and then Dad looked upset and he said, "Now, now ..." and then he hugged Mom and he said he was a great brute, and Mom said she was in the wrong, and Dad said no, he was in the wrong, and they started to laugh and they hugged each other and they hugged me and they told me it was all just a joke, and Mom said she'd go and make some French fries.

And supper was really great, and everyone was smiling like anything, and suddenly Dad said, "You know, darling, I think we were a little hard on old Billings! I'll just ring him and ask him to drop in for coffee and a game of checkers."

Mr. Billings was looking a little suspicious when he arrived.
"You're not going to start arguing again, are you?" he said,
but Mom and Dad just laughed, and they each took him by
one arm and led him into the living room. Dad put the
checkerboard on the little table, Mom brought in the coffee,
and I had a lump of sugar.

And then Dad glanced up. He looked very surprised.

"Hey!" he said. "Where's the pink vase gone?"

Fighting in Recess

"You're a liar," I told Geoffrey.

"Say that again," said Geoffrey.

"You're a liar," I told him.

"Oh, I am, am I?" he asked me.

"Yes," I said, "you are," and the bell went for the end of recess.

"OK," said Geoffrey, as we got in line, "we'll have a fight at next recess, right?"

"Right!" I said, because you won't find me dodging a challenge! Oh, no!

"Silence there!" shouted Old Spuds, who was on duty. It's best not to play him up.

Next lesson was Geography. Alec, who was sitting beside me, said he'd hold my coat for me when I fought Geoffrey at recess, and he advised me to hit him on the chin the way boxers do on TV.

"No, you want to punch him on the nose!" said Eddie, who was sitting behind us. "One good punch, wham! and you've won."

"Wrong!" said Rufus, who was next to Eddie. "Smack his face – that's what Geoffrey doesn't like."

"Fool! How often have you seen boxers smacking each other's faces?" asked Max, who was sitting fairly close to us, and he passed a note to Jeremy, who wanted to know what it was all about, only from where he was sitting he couldn't hear.

Unfortunately, the note happened to reach Cuthbert and Cuthbert is teacher's pet, and he put up his hand and said, "Please, miss, I've got a note."

Our teacher looked surprised, and she asked Cuthbert to bring her the note, and Cuthbert went up to the front looking very pleased with himself. Our teacher read the note, and she said, "It seems that two of you are planning to fight during recess. I don't know what about, and I don't want to know. But I warn you, I shall ask Mr. Goodman after recess, and the culprits will be severely punished. Alec, come up to the blackboard!"

So Alec got asked about the rivers of France, and he wasn't very good because the only ones he knew were the Seine which flows through Paris and the Loire where he went on vacation last year. All our gang could hardly wait for next recess; they were arguing like mad, and our teacher had to bang the table with her ruler and Matthew, who was asleep, thought it was meant for him and went to stand in the corner. I was worried, because if our teacher gave me

detention there'd be trouble at home and I probably wouldn't get any of the chocolate mousse we were having for dessert. Or suppose our teacher had me expelled? That would be awful; Mom would be terribly sad, and Dad would tell me how at my age he was an example to his little friends and what was the use of working his fingers to the bone to give me a good education and I'd come to a bad end and it would be quite some time before I saw the inside of a cinema again. I had a big lump in my throat, and the bell went for the end of the lesson, and I looked at Geoffrey, and I realised he didn't seem to be in any hurry to go down to the playground, either.

Out there, all the gang were waiting. "Let's go to the far end of the playground," said Max. "We'll be private there."

Geoffrey and I followed the others. Then Matthew turned round and said to Cuthbert, "Not you! You told on them!"

"But I want to watch!" said Cuthbert, and then he said that if he couldn't watch, he was going to go and tell Old Spuds this minute, and no one would be able to fight, and it jolly well served us right.

"Oh, let him watch!" said Rufus. "After all, Geoffrey and Nicholas are going to get punished anyway, so it doesn't make any difference whether Cuthbert goes and tells on them before or afterward."

"We'll get punished," said Geoffrey. "We'll get punished if we fight, Nicholas. For the last time, do you take back what you said?"

"Don't be so daft! He isn't taking anything back!" said Alec.

"Oh, no!" said Max.

"Right, off you go," said Eddie. "I'll referee the fight."

"You, be ref?" said Rufus. "Don't make me laugh! Why should you be ref?"

"Don't let's quarrel over that!" said Jeremy. "We'd better get a move on. Recess will soon be over."

"Excuse me," said Geoffrey, "but the ref is very important. I'm not fighting unless there's a good ref!"

"Hear, hear!" I said. "Geoffrey's dead right."

"OK, OK," said Rufus. "I'll be ref."

Eddie didn't care for that, and he said Rufus didn't know the first thing about boxing – he even thought boxers smacked each other's faces.

"A smack from me is every bit as good as a punch on the nose from you!" said Rufus, and wham! he smacked Eddie's face. Eddie was furious, I've never seen him so furious before, and he started fighting Rufus, and he tried to punch his nose, but Rufus wouldn't keep still and that made Eddie even angrier and he kept shouting that Rufus was a rotten sport.

"Stop it! Stop it!" yelled Alec. "Recess will soon be over."

"Why don't you shut your big mouth, fatso?" asked Max.

So Alec asked me to hold his croissant for him, and he started fighting Max. I was really surprised at that, because Alec doesn't usually like fighting, specially not when he's eating a croissant. The thing is that Alec's Mom made him take some kind of slimming pills, and ever since then he hasn't liked being called fatso. I was busy watching Alec and Max, so I don't know why Jeremy kicked Matthew, but I think it could have been because Matthew won a lot of marbles off Jeremy yesterday.

Anyway, all the gang were fighting like mad. It was terrific! I started eating Alec's croissant and I gave a bit of it to Geoffrey. Then Old Spuds came hurrying up and he separated everyone, saying it was disgraceful and we'd see what we would see, and he went to ring the bell.

"There! What did I tell you?" said Alec. "All this fooling around, and Geoffrey and Nicholas didn't even have time for their fight!"

When Old Spuds told her what had happened, our teacher was very cross, and she gave the whole class detention except for Cuthbert and Geoffrey and me, and she said we were an example to the rest, who were disgusting little savages.

"You were dead lucky the bell went!" said Geoffrey. "I could hardly wait to start fighting you!"

"Don't make me laugh!" I said. "Dirty liar!"

"Say that again!" said Geoffrey.

"Dirty liar!" I said.

"Right!" said Geoffrey. "We'll have a fight next recess."

"OK," I said.

Because, let me tell you, you won't find me dodging a challenge. Oh, no!

King

We had decided to go fishing: me and Alec and Eddie and Rufus and Matthew and the rest of the gang.

There is a park close by where we often go to play, and there's this fantastic pond in the park. It has tadpoles in it. Tadpoles are little things that grow up and turn into frogs; we knew that from school. At least, Matthew didn't, because he doesn't often listen in class, but the rest of us had heard about tadpoles.

I got an empty jam jar from home and went off to the park, making sure the park keeper didn't see me. The park keeper has a big mustache and a stick and a whistle just like Rufus's Dad's – he's a policeman – and the park keeper is always telling us off because there are lots of things you aren't allowed to do in the park, like walking on the grass, climbing trees, picking flowers, riding bikes, playing football, dropping candy wrappers, and fighting. We manage to have a good time, all the same.

Eddie, Rufus, and Matthew were already at the pond with their jam jars. Alec was the last to arrive. He explained that he couldn't find an empty jar, so he had to clear one out. His face was still covered with jam and he looked very happy. The park keeper wasn't around, so we started fishing right away.

It's very tricky, fishing for tadpoles. You have to lie flat at the edge of the pond, dip your jar into the water, and try to catch them, but they will keep moving and they don't seem all that keen on swimming into the jam jars. The first to catch a tadpole was Matthew, and he was awfully proud of himself, because he isn't used to being first at anything. In the end, we each had a tadpole. That is, Alec didn't manage to catch one himself, but Rufus is great at fishing and he had two in his jar, so he gave the little one to Alec.

"What do we do with our tadpoles now?" asked Matthew.

"Er, well … we take them home," said Rufus. "And we wait for them to grow up and turn into frogs, and then we'll get them to run races. It'll be fun!"

"Frogs' legs with garlic are simply delicious," said Alec. And he looked at his tadpole and licked his lips.

Then we went off in a hurry, because we saw the park keeper coming. As I walked along the road I kept looking at my tadpole in the jar, and he was really great; he was moving about the whole time, and I was sure he'd turn into a superfrog and win all the races. I decided to call him King after the white horse I saw in a Western at the movies last Saturday. This horse galloped ever so fast, and he came when the cowboy whistled. I thought: I'm going to teach my tadpole tricks, and when he's a frog he'll come when I whistle.

When I got home, Mom looked at me and started screeching: "Just look at you! How did you get into that state?

44

You're covered in mud, and sopping wet, too! What have you been up to this time?"

She was right, I wasn't too clean, specially since I'd forgotten to roll up my shirtsleeves when I put my arms into the pond.

"And what have you got in that jam jar?" asked Mom.

"It's King," I told her, showing her my tadpole. "He's going to turn into a frog and come when I whistle and win races!"

Mom's nose was all wrinkled up.

"Disgusting!" she said. "How many times do I have to tell you not to bring dirty little creatures like that into the house?"

"He isn't dirty," I said, "he's ever so clean, he spends all his time in the water, and I'm going to teach him tricks."

"Well, here comes your father," said Mom. "We'll see what he has to say about it!"

And when Dad saw the jam jar, he said, "Well, well, well, a tadpole," and he sat down in his armchair to read the paper. Mom was very cross.

"Is that all you can find to say?" she asked Dad. "I won't have Nicholas bringing dirty little creatures into the house!"

"Oh, surely, a tadpole isn't much bother," said Dad.

"I see!" said Mom. "I see! Well, since my feelings count for nothing, I'm not saying another word. I warn you, though, it's that tadpole or me!"

And Mom went off to the kitchen.

Dad heaved a deep sigh and folded up his paper.

"I don't think we really have much choice, Nicholas," he said. "We shall have to get rid of this tadpole."

I started to cry, and I said I didn't want anyone hurting King and we were great friends already. Dad put me on his knee.

"Listen, old chap," he said. "You know, this little tadpole has a mommy frog. And the mommy frog must be very sad about losing her little tadpole. Your Mommy wouldn't be pleased if anyone took you away in a jam jar. Well, it's the same with frogs. I tell you what we'll do: you and I will go and put the tadpole back where you found him, and then you can go and see him every Sunday. And I'll buy you a chocolate bar on our way home."

I thought for a bit and then I said OK.

So Dad went off to the kitchen and he told Mom, making a big joke of it, that we'd decided to keep her and let the tadpole go.

Mom laughed too, and hugged me, and said she'd make a *gâteau* for supper, and I felt a lot better.

When we got to the park I showed Dad, who was carrying the jam jar, the way to the pond. "There it is," I said. So then I said goodbye to King, and Dad tipped the contents of the jar into the water.

And then we turned around to go home, and we saw the park keeper coming out from behind a tree, looking very surprised.

"Whether you lot are all crazy or it's me going off my rocker, I don't know," said the park keeper. "But you're the seventh gentleman today, including a policeman, to come and tip a jam jar into the pond at this identical spot!"

My Camera

Just as I was setting off for school, the mailman brought a parcel for me. It was a present from Granny – a camera! My Granny is the best Granny in the whole world!

"Your mother has some pretty funny ideas!" Dad told Mom. "What a present to give a child!" Mom was annoyed, and she said that Dad never approved of anything her mother (my Granny) did, and it was wrong to talk like that in front of little Nicholas, and it was a wonderful present, and I asked if I could take my camera to school and Mom said, yes, but mind I didn't get it confiscated. Dad shrugged his shoulders, and then he and I looked at the instructions and he showed me how to work it. It was dead easy.

At school I showed my camera to Alec, who was sitting next to me, and I said we'd take lots of photographs at recess. So Alec turned around to tell Eddie and Rufus, who were sitting behind us. They told Geoffrey, who passed a note to Max, who handed it to Jeremy, who woke up Matthew, and our teacher said, "Nicholas, perhaps you'll be kind enough to tell me what I have just been saying." So then I stood up and I started to cry because I hadn't the faintest idea what our teacher had just been saying; while she was talking I'd been busy looking at Alec through the little window thing of the camera. "What's

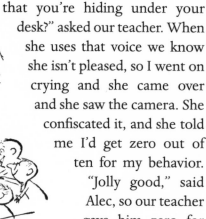

that you're hiding under your desk?" asked our teacher. When she uses that voice we know she isn't pleased, so I went on crying and she came over and she saw the camera. She confiscated it, and she told me I'd get zero out of ten for my behavior. "Jolly good," said Alec, so our teacher gave him zero for behavior too, and told him to stop eating in class, which made me laugh because Alec does eat all the time, she's quite right. "Please, miss," said Cuthbert, who is top of the class and teacher's pet. "I can tell you what you were saying." And the lesson went on. When the bell rang for recess, our teacher made me stay behind after the others and she said, "Now, Nicholas, I don't want to make you unhappy and I can see this is a lovely present. So if you promise to be good and work hard, and not play up in class anymore, I'll forget about that zero for behavior and give you back your camera." I promised like anything, so then our teacher gave me back the camera and told me to go and join my little friends in the playground. I'll tell you something about our teacher: she's great, absolutely great!

When I got out in the playground the gang all gathered round. "We weren't expecting you," said Alec, who was eating a roll and butter. "She's given you back your camera, too!" said

Jeremy. "Yes, and now we'll take some photos," I said. "Everyone get into a group!" So all the gang piled up in front of me, even Cuthbert.

The trouble was, the instructions said to stand four paces away, and my legs are still rather short. So Max measured out the distance for me, because he has very long legs with big dirty knees, and then he went and stood with the others. I looked through the little window thing to see if they were all in the picture; I couldn't get Eddie's head in because he's too tall, and half of Cuthbert was cut off, the right half. It was a pity about the sandwich hiding Alec's face, but he didn't want to stop eating. They all smiled and I went click! and took the picture. I knew it would be great!

"That's a fantastic camera!" said Eddie. "Huh!" said Geoffrey. "I've got a much better one at home, one my Dad bought me, with a flash." Everyone started laughing; honestly, Geoffrey will say anything! "What does a flash do?" I asked. "Well, it's a bright light that goes whoosh! like a firework, and you can take photos in the dark," said Geoffrey. "I don't think so," I said, "nobody can take photos in the dark, you're a liar!" "Want a smack in the face?" asked Geoffrey. "I can hold your camera for you if you like, Nicholas," said Alec. So I gave him my camera, telling him to be careful; I was a bit worried because his fingers

were all buttery and I was afraid they might slip. We started fighting, and Old Spuds, who was on playground duty but that isn't his real name, came running up and separated us. "What's going on now?" he asked. "It's Nicholas," said Alec, "he's fighting Geoffrey because his camera doesn't have fireworks to go off in the dark."

"Don't talk with your mouth full," said Old Spuds, "and what's all this nonsense about a camera?"

So Alec gave him the camera, and Old Spuds said he had a good mind to confiscate it. "Oh, please, sir, no, sir!" I said. "Very well," said Old Spuds, "you can keep it, but you must be good and not fight any more, understand? Look me in the eye, boy!" So I did, and I said I understood, and then I asked if I could take a picture of him.

Old Spuds looked very surprised. "You want a picture of me?" he asked. "Yes, please, sir," I said. Old Spuds smiled, and when he smiles he really looks quite nice. "Well, well, well!" he said. "All right, but hurry up, because I must ring the bell for the end of recess." And then Old Spuds stood perfectly still in the middle of the playground with one hand in his pocket and the other on his chest and one foot forward, looking straight ahead of him into the distance. Max counted out the four paces for me, and I looked at Old Spuds through the little window, and he looked terribly funny. I went click! and took the photo and then he went to ring the bell.

At home that evening, when Dad got back from the office, I told him I wanted to take a picture of him and Mom. "Oh, Nicholas, I'm tired," said Dad. "Put that camera away and let me read my paper." "Don't be so unkind," Mom told him. "Why spoil the child's fun? His photographs will be delightful souvenirs for him." Dad sighed heavily and stood beside Mom, and I took the last six pictures on the film. Mom hugged me, and told me I was her own dear little photographer.

Next day, Dad took the film away to get it developed. We had to wait several days to see the pictures, and I was getting ever so impatient. And then yesterday evening Dad brought them home.

"Not bad," said Dad, "at least, the ones you took at school of your friends and the old boy with the mustache ... the ones you took at home have come out darker, but they're the funniest!" Mom came to look, and Dad showed her the photographs and said, "I must say, your son doesn't exactly flatter you!" and he laughed, and Mom took the photographs and said it was time for supper.

What I don't understand is why Mom changed her mind. Because now she says Dad was right, a camera is not the kind of toy to give a little boy.

And she's put my camera right at the top of the closet.

Our Soccer Team

I was out on the bit of waste ground with the rest of the gang: Eddie, Geoffrey, Alec, Cuthbert, Rufus, Matthew, Max, and Jeremy. I'm not sure if I've already told you about our gang, but I know I mentioned the waste ground. It's a fantastic place, full of old cans, stones, cats, bits of wood, and an automobile. The car doesn't have any wheels, but it's good fun: you can sit in it and go "vrrrooom, vrrrooom!" and play buses and planes, and it's really great.

But we weren't going to play with the car today, we were going to play soccer. Alec has a soccer ball and he lends it on condition that he can be in goal, because he doesn't like running. Geoffrey, who has this very rich Dad, had come in his soccer player's outfit with red, white, and blue shirt, white shorts with a red stripe down them, long socks and shin guards, and fantastic boots with studs on the soles, so really it was the rest of us who needed shin guards, because Geoffrey is what they call an aggressive player, specially in those boots.

We'd decided how to form our team: Alec would be in goal, and Eddie and Cuthbert were backs. Nothing gets past Eddie because he's very strong and people are scared of him; he's a very aggressive player, too. And we'd put Cuthbert at the back so he wouldn't get in our way, because we daren't shove him

or thump him on account of his glasses and he cries easily. Rufus, Matthew, and Jeremy were our halfbacks. They had to pass the ball to the forwards. There were only three forwards because we didn't have enough people, but all the same, we had a great forward line: there was Max, who has long legs with big dirty knees and runs very fast, there was me (I'm a fantastic shot at goal), and then there was Geoffrey, with his boots.

We felt very pleased to have formed our team.

"Right, time for kickoff!" shouted Max.

"Pass! Pass!" yelled Jeremy.

We were having a great time, when Geoffrey suddenly said, "Wait a minute, everyone! Who are we playing against? We need an opposing team!"

Geoffrey was right there; it's all very well passing and so on, but it's not much fun if there isn't anyone to score against. I suggested dividing into two teams, but Matthew said, "What, split up our team? Never!" Besides, it was the same as playing Cowboys and Indians: nobody wanted to be on the other side.

And then the boys from the other school turned up. We don't like the boys from the other school, they're a stupid lot. They often come to the waste ground, though, and then we fight; we say the waste ground is ours and they say it's theirs, and that leads to a difference of opinion. This time, however, we were quite pleased to see them.

"Hey, you!" I said. "Want to play soccer with us? We've got a ball."

"Play soccer with you? Don't make us laugh!" said one thin boy with red hair like Auntie Clarissa's hair, which turned red last month, and Mom explained it was some kind of paint stuff the hairdresser put on it.

"What's so funny, then, idiot?" asked Rufus.

"The thought of the thumping I'm going to give you, that's what!" said the red-haired boy.

"And for a start," said a big boy with a lot of teeth, "push off! This bit of waste ground is ours!"

Cuthbert wanted to push off, but the rest of us didn't.

"Oh, no, it isn't!" said Matthew. "It's ours. You're just scared to play soccer with us. We've got a fabulous team!"

"A feeble-ass team! Hee-haw!" said the toothy boy, making donkey noises, and they all started to laugh, and so did I, because it was a funny joke, and then Eddie punched a little boy on the nose. The little boy wasn't saying anything, but he turned out to be the brother of the big toothy boy, so there was a spot of ill feeling.

"Let's see you do that again!" said the big toothy boy to Eddie.

"You lot are nuts!" said the little boy, who was holding his nose. And Geoffrey kicked the thin boy with hair like Auntie Clarissa's.

Then we all had a fight except Cuthbert, who was crying, and yelping, "My glasses! I've got glasses!" It was really great, and then my Dad turned up.

"You little savages!" shouted Dad. 'I could hear you shouting all the way from home! You, Nicholas! Do you know what the time is?"

And Dad took hold of the great brute who was fighting me by his collar.

"You just leave me alone!" shouted the great brute. "Or I'm fetching my own Dad, and he's a tax inspector, and I'll tell him to make you pay lots and lots of taxes!"

Dad let go of the brute. "All right, that will do!" he said. "It's late, your parents will be getting worried. What were you fighting about, anyway? Can't you play nicely?"

"We were fighting because they're scared to play soccer with us," I said.

"Scared? What, us, scared? Us, scared?" shouted the big boy with all the teeth.

"Well, if you aren't scared, why won't you play?" asked Dad.

"Because they're just weeds, that's why," said the great brute.

"Weeds?" I said. "With a forward line like me and Max and Geoffrey? Don't make me laugh!"

"Geoffrey?" said Dad. "Personally, I'd play him as a defender; I don't know that he's all that fast."

"Wait a minute!" said Geoffrey. "I've got proper boots and I'm the best dressed, so I ought ..."

"Who's in goal?" asked Dad.

So we told him about our team and Dad said it wasn't bad, but we'd have to train properly, and he would be our manager, because he was very nearly a soccer international once (he played inside right for the Chanticleer club), and if he hadn't got married he would have been. I never knew that before. My Dad's terrific!

"Well," said Dad to the boys from the other school, "are you willing to play my team next Sunday? I'll referee the match."

"Them, willing? They're cowards!" shouted Max.

"Oh no, we're not!" said the red-haired boy. "Sunday it is, then! Three o'clock. Just you wait! We're going to murder you!"

And then they left.

Dad stayed with us to start our training. He took a shot at goal and got the ball past Alec. Then he went in goal instead of Alec, and Alec got the ball past him. Then Dad showed us how to pass. He threw in the ball and shouted, "Yours, Matthew! Pass!" And the ball hit Cuthbert, and his glasses fell off, and he started to cry.

Then Mom turned up.

"So there you are!" she said to Dad. "What on earth are you doing? I sent you to look for Nicholas and you never came back, and supper's getting cold!"

Then Dad went bright red and took my hand and said, "Come along, Nicholas, time to go home!" and all the gang shouted, "See you on Sunday! Three cheers for Nicholas's Dad!"

Mom made silly jokes all through supper, and when she wanted to ask Dad for the salt she said, "Come on, pass, Georgie Best!"

Mothers! They don't understand sport. Never mind, next Sunday is going to be the greatest!

The First Half

1. Yesterday afternoon, a soccer match took place on the waste ground between a team from another school and a team trained by Nicholas's father. The latter team was as follows: goalkeeper, Alec; backs, Eddie and Matthew; halfbacks, Jeremy, Rufus, and Cuthbert; inside right, Nicholas; center-forward, Geoffrey; left wing, Max. Referee: Nicholas's father.

2. You will have noticed that there wasn't any right wing or inside left. This shortage of players meant that Nicholas's father had to adopt a tactical approach (perfected during the final training session), which consisted of playing a counter-attacking game. Nicholas, whose qualities of attack are comparable to those of Pelé, and Max, whose qualities of skill and tactical sense are comparable to those of Maradona, were to pass the ball to Geoffrey, whose qualities aren't comparable to those of anyone in particular, but he does own a complete soccer player's kit, which is a good thing for a center-forward.

3. Kickoff was at about 15.40 hours. In the first minute of the game, following a spot of confusion in front of the goal, the other side's left wing kicked such a powerful shot that Alec had to dive desperately to avoid the ball, which was making straight for him. However, the goal was disallowed because the referee remembered that the captains hadn't shaken hands yet.

4. In the fifth minute, while play was going on in midfield, a dog ate Alec's sandwiches even though they were wrapped in three pieces of paper and tied with three bits of string, thus severely injuring the mood of the goalkeeper (and everyone knows how important the goalkeeper's mood is), who let in the first goal of the match in the seventh minute ...

5. And the second goal in the eighth minute ... In the ninth minute, Eddie, as captain, told Alec to go and play on the left wing while Max took his place in goal. (Which, in our considered opinion, was a mistake, Alec being more a midfield player than a forward by nature.)

6. In the fourteenth minute, such a downpour fell on the pitch that most of the players ran for shelter, Nicholas remaining to dispute possession of the ball with a player from the opposing side. No goals were scored during this period.

7. In the twentieth minute, Geoffrey, playing at something like right half or inside left, it doesn't matter which, kicked a tremendous shot right over the touchline.

8. Also in the twentieth minute, the ball hit Mr. Denman, who was off to visit his sick old granny.

9. The impact threw Mr. Denman off balance, and he swerved into the front yard of a neighbor who was his deadliest enemy.

10. He soon appeared on the pitch, having taken a brilliant shortcut, and took possession of the ball just as it was about to be put back into play.

11. After five minutes of confusion, thus bringing us to the twenty-fifth minute, the match continued, with a can instead of the ball.

In the twenty-sixth, twenty-seventh, and twenty-eighth minutes, Alec, thanks to some superb dribbling, scored three goals (it's practically impossible to get a can of top quality garden peas, even an empty one, away from Alec). Nicholas's team was leading 3–2.

12. In the thirtieth minute, Mr. Denman came back with the ball. (His old granny was better and he had mended his glasses with sticky tape.) As the can was of no more use, it was thrown away.

13. In the thirty-first minute, Nicholas penetrated the opposition's defense, passed the ball to Rufus who was playing inside left (only, as there wasn't any inside left, he was in the center-forward position), Rufus passed to Matthew who, shooting to the left, took everyone by surprise and hit the referee in the stomach. The referee, in a faint voice, told the two captains that as the sky was clouding over and it looked like more rain and the air was rather cool now, it would be better to play the second half next week.

The Second Half

1. In the course of the week, telephone calls between Nicholas's father and the other fathers resulted in considerable changes to the team: Eddie went to inside left and Geoffrey to back. Several tactical maneuvers were perfected at a fathers' meeting. The chief one consisted in the scoring of a goal during the first few minutes, then playing defensively, then taking advantage of a counterattack to score again. If the boys followed these instructions to the letter, they would win the match 5–2, since they were already leading 3–2. The fathers (Nicholas's father, the fathers of the rest of the gang, and the fathers of the boys from the other school) were present in full force at kickoff, which occurred, amidst great suspense, at 16.03 hours.

2. Out on the pitch, you couldn't hear a thing but advice from the fathers. This put the players off. For the first few minutes, nothing much happened except for a shot from Rufus which hit Max's Dad in the back, and a smack in the face which Matthew got from his own father for missing a pass. Jeremy, who was captain at the moment (it had been decided that the players would all be captain for five minutes each), went to ask the referee to get the ground cleared. Matthew said the smack in the face had shaken him up so much that he couldn't play

anymore. His father said right, he'd play instead. The boys from the other school objected, and said in that case they'd have their fathers on the field too.

3. A ripple of pleasurable anticipation ran through the fathers, all of whom took off their coats and jackets and scarves and hats. They ran onto the pitch, telling the boys to watch carefully and not come too close, and they'd show them the right way to play soccer.

4. From the very first minute or so of the match between the fathers of Nicholas's gang and the fathers of the boys from the other school, their sons had got the hang of the right way to play soccer …

5. … and decided by common consent to go home to Matthew's house and watch 'The Big Match' on his color TV.

6. The match continued, care being taken by some of the players to take great swipes at the ball in order to prove that a goal could easily be scored if it wasn't for the wind blowing the wrong way in all directions at once. In the sixteenth minute, a father from the other school kicked the ball hard in the direction of a father whom he hoped was another father from the other school, but actually it was Geoffrey's father. Geoffrey's father kicked it even harder. The ball came down in the middle of an assortment of crates, cans, and bits of old iron. A noise like that of a soccer ball deflating was heard, but the ball bounced back again, thanks to an old spring which had passed right through it. After three seconds of discussion it was decided to continue the game with a can instead of the ball (and why not?).

7. In the thirty-sixth minute, Rufus's father, playing back, stopped the can, which was flying through the air toward his upper lip. Since he stopped it with his hand, the referee (the brother of one of the fathers of the boys from the other school, as Nicholas's father was now playing inside right) blew the whistle and awarded a penalty. Despite the protests of some of the players, i.e. Nicholas's father and the fathers of the rest of the gang, the penalty was taken, and Matthew's father, in goal, was unable to keep the can out, in spite of a gesture of annoyance. The fathers of the boys from the other school had thus equalized, the score being 3–3.

8. There were still a few minutes of play left. All the fathers were worried about what their sons would say if they lost the match. Play, which until now had been only bad, now became excruciating. The fathers of the boys from the other school were playing a defensive game. Some of them stood on the can with both feet to stop anyone else from getting it. Suddenly, Rufus's father, who is a policeman in private life, managed to get it away. Dribbling past two of the opposing fathers, he found himself alone in front of the goal, took aim, shot, and put the can right into the goal. The fathers of Nicholas and his gang won 4–3.

9. Photograph of the winning team, taken after the game. Standing, left to right: the fathers of Max, Rufus (the hero of the match), Eddie (injured in the left eye), Geoffrey, and Alec. Sitting: the fathers of Jeremy, Matthew, Nicholas (injured in the left eye owing to a collision with Eddie's father), and Cuthbert.

The Art Gallery

I was feeling very happy today because our teacher was going to take the whole class to the art gallery. It's great fun when we have one of these outings, and I wish our teacher would do it more often; it's a pity she won't. All the same, she's OK.

We were going from school to the art gallery in a coach. The coach couldn't pull up outside the school building, so we had to cross the road. Our teacher said, "Get into a line and hold hands with a partner, and mind you're careful!" I wasn't so keen on this because I was next to my friend Alec, who is very fat and eats all the time, and it's not very nice holding hands with him. I like Alec all right, but his hands are always greasy or sticky, according to what he's been eating. I was lucky today, though, his hands were quite dry. "What have you got to eat, Alec?" I asked. "Cookies," he said, blowing a whole lot of cookie crumbs in my face.

Cuthbert was walking at the front beside our teacher. He's top of the class and teacher's pet and we aren't mad about him, but we can't thump him as much as we'd like because of his glasses. "Come on, everyone!" shouted Cuthbert, and we started crossing the road while a policeman held up the traffic to let us over.

All of a sudden Alec let go of my hand and said he'd be back in a minute, he'd left his candy in the classroom. And he began to cross the road in the opposite direction from the rest of us, barging right through the middle of the line of boys, which made for a bit of upheaval. "Alec, where are you going?" shouted our teacher. "Come back this minute!" "That's right, Alec, where are you going?" said Cuthbert. "Come back this minute!" Eddie didn't fancy Cuthbert's tone; Eddie is very strong and he likes to punch people's noses. "What are you shoving your oar in for? Soppy old teacher's pet!" said Eddie, advancing on Cuthbert. "Want a punch on the nose?" Cuthbert got behind our teacher and said Eddie couldn't hit him because he wore glasses. So then Eddie started pushing past everyone (he was at the back of the line on account of being so tall) because he wanted to get at Cuthbert and take his glasses off and then punch him on the nose. "Eddie, get back to your place!" said our teacher. "That's right, Eddie," said Cuthbert, "get back to your place!" "Listen, I don't like to bother you," said the policeman, "but I've been holding up the traffic for some time now, so if you intend to teach these kids their lesson right here on the pedestrian crossing, just let me know and I'll redirect the cars through the school!" We'd have loved to watch him do that, but our teacher went all red, and from the way she told us to get into the coach this minute, we could see this was no time to act up. We got in, quick.

The coach started, and behind it the policeman began waving the traffic on, and then we heard a squeal of brakes and some shouting. It was Alec, running across the road clutching his bag of candy.

Finally, Alec got into the coach and we were able to start off. Before we turned the corner of the road, I saw the policeman

throwing his white gloves
down on the ground in the
middle of a whole lot of cars
that had bumped into each
other.

We filed into the art gallery,
being very good, because
we're fond of our teacher and
we'd noticed that she seemed
all worked up today, like
Mom when Dad drops
cigarette ash on the carpet.
We went into a big room
with masses of pictures
hanging on the walls.
"Here you will see
pictures painted by the
great masters of the
Flemish School," our
teacher began to tell us,
but she wasn't able to carry
on for long because an attendant
came running up, shouting because Alec
had rubbed his fingers over one picture to see if the paint was
still wet. The attendant said we mustn't touch, and he started
arguing with Alec, who was saying that we could touch,
because the paint was quite dry so there wasn't any danger of
messing it up. Our teacher told Alec to be quiet and she
promised the attendant to keep an eye on us. The attendant
went off, shaking his head.

While our teacher went on explaining, we slid; it was great fun, because the floor was all shiny tiles which were very good for making slides. We all did slides, except for our teacher, who had her back to us and was talking about a picture, and Cuthbert, who was standing beside her, listening and taking notes. Alec wasn't playing, either. He'd stopped in front of a little picture of some fish and steaks and fruit. Alec was looking at this picture, licking his lips.

We were having a lot of fun, and Eddie did some really fantastic slides. He could slide almost the whole length of the room. After the slides we started a game of leapfrog, but we had to stop because Cuthbert turned round and said, "Oh, look, miss, they're mucking about!" Eddie was cross and he went over to Cuthbert, who had taken off his glasses to wipe them, so he didn't see Eddie coming. It wasn't Cuthbert's lucky day; if he hadn't taken off his glasses, he wouldn't have got his nose punched.

The attendant came back and he asked our teacher if she didn't think it would be better for us to leave now. Our teacher said yes, she'd had about enough of this.

We were just going to leave the art gallery when Alec went up to the attendant. He had the little picture he liked so much under his arm, the one of the fish and steaks and fruit, and he said he'd like to buy it. He wanted to know how much the attendant was asking.

When we'd left the art gallery, Geoffrey told our teacher that if she was so fond of pictures, she could come to his house some time, because his Mom and Dad had a marvelous collection, everybody knew about it. Our teacher put her hand in front of her eyes and she said she never wanted to see another picture again as long as she lived, she didn't even want to hear about pictures.

So then I realized why our teacher hadn't looked very happy about spending the day in the art gallery with us. She isn't really very fond of pictures at all.

The March Past

They're going to unveil a statue near our school, and we're going to march past. That's what the Principal told us when he came into our classroom this morning and we all stood up, except for Matthew, who was asleep and got told off. Matthew was very surprised to be woken up and told he'd have detention after school. He started to cry and that made a lot of noise and personally I think they might just as well have let him go on sleeping.

"Now, boys," said the Principal, "there will be representatives of the Government at the unveiling ceremony, and a company of soldiers to pay the military honors, and the pupils of this school are to have the privilege of marching past the monument and laying a wreath at the foot of it. I'm counting on you to behave like perfect little gentlemen." And then the Principal told us that the big boys were rehearsing for the march past now, and we'd rehearse after them, in the last lesson of the morning. Since the last lesson is Grammar we all thought this march past idea was great. When the Principal had left the room we all started talking at once, and then our teacher banged her desk with the ruler and we did math.

When it was time for the Grammar lesson, our teacher sent us out into the playground, where the Principal and Old Spuds were waiting for us. Old Spuds is one of the teachers, and we call him that because he's always saying, "Boy, look me in the eye!" and potatoes have eyes, but I think I told you about that before.

"Well, here we are, Mr. Goodman!" said the Principal. "I hope you'll be as successful with them as you were with the big boys just now." Mr. Goodman (that's what the Principal calls Old Spuds) began to laugh, and he said he'd been in the Army in his time, he'd soon teach some drill and how to march in step. "Don't worry, you won't know them for the same boys when I've done with them!" said Old Spuds. "If only that were true!" said the Principal, and he sighed, deeply, and went off.

"Right!" said Old Spuds. "Now, when getting into position for a march past we need one man called a guide. The guide stands to attention and everyone else gets in line with him. Usually the tallest man is picked. Understand?" And then he looked at us and pointed to Max and said, "You, boy – you can be the guide." So Eddie said, "Please, sir, he isn't the tallest, sir, he only looks the tallest because of his enormous long legs, but I'm taller than he is really." "Don't be such a silly nit," said Max. "I am taller than you, and what's more, my Auntie Alice who came to see us yesterday said I'd grown since she last saw me. I'm growing the whole time." "Want to bet on it?" said Eddie, and so they stood back to back, but we never did know

who won the bet, because Old Spuds started to shout at us to form lines of three any way we liked, and that took an awful lot of time. And then, when we were in line, Old Spuds stood in front of us and closed one eye, and then he waved his hand about and said, "You! Over to the left a little. Nicholas, you're too far to the left, move to the right. You! You're too far to the right!" The funny part was when he got to Alec, because Alec is very fat and he was too far to the left and to the right. When Old Spuds had finished, he looked pleased, he rubbed his hands, he turned his back to us and he shouted, "Section! At the word of command ..." "Please, sir, about this wreath," said Rufus. "The one we're going to lay at the foot of the monument. What's it made of?"

"Flowers, of course," said Cuthbert. "Silence in the ranks!" shouted Old Spuds. "Section, at the word of command ..." "Please, sir," called Max, "Eddie is standing on tiptoe so as to look taller than me. He's cheating!" "Dirty sneak!" said Eddie, and he punched Max's nose, and Max kicked Eddie, and we all gathered round to watch because it's a fantastic sight when Eddie and Max are having a fight; they're the strongest in the class. Old Spuds came over, and he parted Eddie and Max and gave them both detention.

By now Matthew was facing the wrong way, and Old Spuds gave him detention, too. Of course, Old Spuds wasn't to know that Matthew had been given detention already.

Old Spuds passed his hand over his face, and then he got us all back into line, and I have to admit that wasn't easy because we were moving about rather a lot. And then Old Spuds glared at us for a long, long time, and we could see this was not the moment to act up. Then Old Spuds stepped backward, and Jeremy was just coming up behind him and he trod on Jeremy's toes. "Watch out, can't you?"

said Jeremy. Old Spuds went bright red. "Where did you spring from?" he shouted. "I went to get a drink of water while Max and Eddie were fighting, sir," Jeremy explained. "I thought it would last longer than this." And Old Spuds gave him detention, too, and told him to get back into line.

"Now, all of you, look me in the eye!" said Old Spuds. "The first boy to make a movement or say a word gets expelled from school, understand?" And then Old Spuds turned round and raised one arm and shouted, "Section, at the word of command – forward … march!" And, holding himself very stiffly, Old Spuds took several steps, and then he looked behind him, and when he saw we were all still standing in the same place, I thought he was going to hit the roof, like Mr. Billings next door when Dad sprayed him with our hosepipe over the hedge last Sunday. "Why didn't you obey?" asked Old Spuds. "Please, you told us not to move, sir," said Geoffrey. Then Old Spuds really let fly. "Oh, I'm really going to murder you, I am!" he shouted. "You horrible little boys, you! You're going to get the thrashing of your lives!" And several of us started to cry, and the Principal came out at the run.

"Really, Mr. Goodman, I could hear you from my office!" said the Principal. "Is this any way to address young children? You're not in the Army now, you know." "The Army?" said Old Spuds. "Let me tell you, the roughest bunch of recruits I ever laid eyes on were angelic choirboys, they really were, compared to this lot!" And Old Spuds went off, making a lot of wild movements with his hands, followed by the Principal saying, "Now, now, Goodman, calm down, old fellow!"

The unveiling of the statue was fantastic, but the Principal had changed his mind and we didn't march past after all, we sat on some seats behind the soldiers. It was a shame Old Spuds couldn't be there, but apparently he's gone to stay with his family in the country for two weeks to have a rest.

The Boy Scouts

Our gang all clubbed together to buy our teacher a present, because it's her birthday tomorrow. First, we counted the money. Cuthbert, who is best at arithmetic, did the sum. We were pleased, because Geoffrey had brought five thousand old francs which his Dad had given him. His Dad is very rich and gives him anything he wants.

"We've got five thousand, two hundred, and seven francs," said Cuthbert. "We can buy a really nice present with that."

The trouble was, we didn't know what to get. "We could give her a box of candy, or a whole lot of little chocolate croissants," said Alec, my fat friend who is always eating. But the rest of us said no, because if we got her something to eat we'd all want a taste and there wouldn't be anything left for our teacher. "My Dad bought my Mom a fur coat, and my Mom was very pleased," said Geoffrey. That sounded like a good idea, but Geoffrey said it must have cost more than five thousand, two hundred, and seven francs, because his Mom really had been very, very pleased. "How about buying her a book?" asked Cuthbert. That really made us laugh. Cuthbert is nuts! "Or a fountain pen?" said Eddie. But Matthew objected; Matthew is bottom of the class, and he said he didn't fancy the idea of our teacher writing down his rotten marks with a pen he'd paid for. "Listen, there's a gift shop near my house," said Rufus. "They've got some fantastic things. I'm sure we'll find a present there." That seemed a good idea, and we decided we'd all go to the gift shop together after school.

When we got to the gift shop, we looked in the window; it was fantastic, as Rufus said. There were lots of fabulous things: little statuettes and salad bowls made of sort of crinkly glass and decanters like the one we never use at home and lots of little knives and forks and even clocks. But the best things were the statuettes. There was one of a man in his underpants trying to stop two horses who didn't want to stop, and another of a lady shooting with a bow; the bow didn't have any string but it looked so good you'd have thought it did, and it looked lovely with the statuette of a lion with an arrow in its back, dragging its hind legs. And there were two black tigers prowling, and some models of Boy Scouts, and little dogs and elephants, and a man in the shop looking at us as if he didn't like the sight of us much.

When we went inside, the man came to meet us, waving his hands around.

"Now then, now then, out you go!" he said. "This isn't a funfair, you know."

"We didn't come to have fun," said Alec. "We want to buy a present."

"A present for our teacher," I said.

"We've got money," said Geoffrey.

And Cuthbert took the five thousand, two hundred, and

seven francs out of his pocket and showed them to the man, who said, "All right, but don't touch anything."

"How much is that?" asked Matthew, picking up a statue of two horses which was on the counter.

"Careful! Leave that alone, it's fragile!" shouted the man, and he was quite right to worry, because Matthew is very clumsy and always breaking things. Matthew was annoyed, but he put the statue back again, and the man was just in time to catch an elephant which Matthew had knocked over with his elbow.

We looked all around the shop, and the man ran after us shouting, "Don't touch, don't touch! That's breakable!" I felt sorry for the man. It must be nerve-racking, working in a shop where everything is breakable. Finally, the man asked us all to stand together in the middle of the room with our hands behind our backs and tell him what we wanted to buy.

"What can we have for five thousand, two hundred, and seven francs? Something really nice," said Jeremy. The man looked round, and then he took two models of Boy Scouts out of the window. You might have thought they were real. I've never seen anything so beautiful, not even at the rifle range at the fair.

"You can have these for five thousand francs," said the man.

"That's less than we expected to pay," said Cuthbert.

"I'd rather have the horses," said Matthew.

And Matthew was going to pick the horses up again, but the man got there first and picked them up off the counter and cradled them in his arms.

"Well, do you want the Boy Scouts or don't you?" said the man. He seemed to be in no mood for any nonsense, so we said OK. Cuthbert gave him the five thousand old francs and we went out with the Boy Scouts.

Out in the road we started arguing about who would look after the present and give it to our teacher in the morning.

"Me," said Geoffrey. "I gave most money."

"I'm top of the class," said Cuthbert, "so I ought to give her the present."

"You're teacher's pet, that's all you are," said Rufus.

Cuthbert started to cry and say he was very unhappy, but he didn't roll about on the ground like he usually does, because he was holding the Boy Scouts and he didn't want to break them. While Rufus, Eddie, Geoffrey, and Jeremy were fighting, I got the idea of tossing for it. That took quite a bit of time, and we lost two coins down a drain, and in the end Matthew won. We weren't too pleased, because Matthew breaks so many things we were afraid our teacher would never get her present at all. Still, we handed the Boy Scouts over to Matthew, and Eddie told him that if he broke them, he, Eddie, would punch his nose, a lot of times. Matthew promised to take great care of them, and he went home carrying the present, walking very carefully with his tongue sticking out. The rest of us bought little chocolate croissants with the two hundred and seven francs we had left, lots of them, and we weren't hungry for supper and our parents thought we must be sick.

We were all pretty worried when we got to school next day, but we were relieved to see Matthew arrive carrying the Boy Scouts. "I didn't sleep a wink all night," said Matthew. "I was afraid they might fall off my bedside table."

When we were in the classroom, I looked at Matthew, who had put the present under his desk and was keeping an eye on it. I was terribly jealous, because when Matthew gave our teacher her present she'd be very pleased and hug him, and

Matthew would go all red, because when our teacher is pleased she looks very pretty, almost as pretty as my Mom.

"What are you hiding under your desk, Matthew?" asked our teacher. And then she went over to Matthew's desk, looking cross. "Come along, out with it!" said our teacher. Matthew gave her the present, and as she looked at it she said, "I've told you before not to bring rubbish like this to school! I'm confiscating these until the end of the day, and you'll be kept in after school!"

And then, when we wanted to go and get our money back, we couldn't, because Matthew went and slipped outside the shop, and the Boy Scouts got broken.

Matthew's Arm

Matthew trod on his little red truck at home, and he fell over and broke his arm. We were very sorry for Matthew, because he's one of our gang, and I knew that little red truck of his, too, it was great, with headlights that really worked, and I shouldn't think anyone would be able to mend it after Matthew trod on it.

We wanted to go and see him at his home, but his mother wouldn't let us in. We told her we were friends of Matthew's and he knew us very well, but Matthew's Mom told us he needed to rest, and she knew us very well, too.

That's why we were so pleased to see Matthew back at school today. He had his arm in a sort of cloth thing round his neck, like in adventure movies when the young hero has been wounded, because in adventure movies the young hero always does get wounded in the arm or in the shoulder, and you'd think those actors who play the young heroes would know about it by now and they'd watch out. We'd been at school for half an hour already, so Matthew went up to our teacher to say he was sorry he was late, but instead of telling him off, she said, "I'm so pleased to see you, Matthew. It's very brave of you to come back to school with your arm in plaster. I do hope it doesn't hurt any more." Matthew's jaw dropped. Being bottom of the class, he isn't used to having our teacher talk to him like that, specially when he's late. He just stood there with his mouth open, and our teacher said, "Go and sit down, dear!"

When Matthew had sat down, we started asking him masses of questions; we asked if it hurt, and what that hard stuff round his arm was, and we said how pleased we were to see him. But then our teacher told us to leave our friend alone, and said she wouldn't allow us to make this an excuse to misbehave. "Huh!" said Geoffrey. "Can't a person even speak to his friends these days?" So our teacher made him stand in the corner, and Matthew laughed fit to bust.

"Now, we'll do some dictation," said our teacher. We got our notebooks out, and Matthew tried to get his out of his satchel with one hand. "I'll help you," said Jeremy, who was sitting next to him. "Nobody asked you to," said Matthew. Our teacher looked at Matthew, and she said, "No, dear, not you, of course! You have a rest." Matthew stopped searching his satchel and looked very unhappy, as if he hated not being able to do dictation. It was a terrible dictation, too, with lots of words like "chrysanthemum" where we all made mistakes, and "dicotyledon," and the only one who got it right was Cuthbert, who is top of the class and teacher's pet. Every time there was a difficult word, I looked at Matthew and he was grinning away.

Then the bell went for recess. Matthew was the first to stand

up. "It might be better for you not to go out into the playground, with that arm of yours," said our teacher. Matthew looked the same as he did over the dictation, only more annoyed. "The doctor said I have to have fresh air or he wouldn't answer for the consequences," said Matthew. Our teacher said all right, but he must be careful. And she made Matthew go out first, so that we couldn't push him on the stairs. Before she let us go down, too, our teacher gave us lots of advice: she told us we must be careful and not play rough games, and protect Matthew so he didn't hurt himself. We lost several minutes of recess, listening to her. When we finally did get down to the playground, we went and looked for Matthew; he was playing leapfrog with some boys from another class, who are all very silly and we don't like them.

We all gathered round Matthew and asked him questions. Matthew seemed very full of himself, being the center of attention like this. We asked if his little red truck was broken, and he said yes, but people had given him lots of presents to cheer him up while he was in bed. He'd got a sailing ship, a game of checkers, two cars, a train, and lots of books that he was willing to swap for other toys. And then he said how nice everyone had been: the doctor brought him candy every time he called, and his Mom and Dad put the TV in his room, and he had masses of nice things to eat. Hearing anyone mention eating makes my fat friend Alec feel very hungry. He found a chocolate bar in his pocket and took a bite out of it. "Hey, can I have a bit of that?" asked Matthew. "No," said Alec. "I've got a bad arm, haven't I?" said Matthew. "Bad arm, my foot!" said Alec. Matthew was upset, and he started howling that people were taking advantage of him because of his broken arm, and we wouldn't treat him like this if he could hit back like anyone else! Matthew howled so loud that the teacher on duty ran over. "What's going on here?" the teacher asked. "He's taking advantage of my broken arm!" said Matthew, pointing to Alec. Alec wasn't one little bit pleased and he tried to say so, but his mouth was so full he just sprayed chocolate everywhere and you couldn't make out a word of it. "Aren't you ashamed of yourself?" said the teacher to Alec. "Taking advantage of a disabled friend! Go and stand in the corner!"

"Yeah!" said Matthew.

"You mean," said Alec, who had finally swallowed his chocolate, "if he breaks an arm fooling about, I have to give him things to eat?"

"Hear, hear!" said Geoffrey. "We only have to speak to him and we get put in the corner. I'm fed up with his silly old arm!"

The teacher on duty looked at us very sadly, and then he spoke in a very soft voice, like when Dad is explaining to Mom how he absolutely has to go to his regimental reunion dinner. "You have no proper feelings!" he told us. "You are still very young, I know, but your attitude saddens me deeply!" He stopped, and then he shouted, "Go and stand in the corner, all of you!"

So we all had to stand in the corner, even Cuthbert. It's the first time he ever did have to, and he didn't know how, so we showed him, and there we all were, except for Matthew, of course. The teacher on duty patted Matthew's head and asked if his arm hurt; Matthew said it did a bit, and then the teacher went to see about a big boy who was using a little boy to hit another big boy. Matthew looked at us for a moment, grinning, and then he went back to his game of leapfrog.

I wasn't at all cheerful when I got home, and Dad, who was

just back from the office, asked me what the matter was. "It's not fair!" I said. "Why can't I ever break my arm?"

Dad stared at me, very surprised, and I went up to my room to sulk.

The Medical Examination

We didn't go to school this morning, but that wasn't any fun because we had to go to the clinic to be examined and to see if we had any illnesses and if we were nuts or not. At school, we'd each been given a piece of paper to take home to our parents, explaining how we had to go to this clinic, along with our vaccination certificates, our mothers, and our school record cards. Our teacher told us we were going to be examined and given a psychological test. A psychological test is when they make you draw little pictures to find out if you're nuts.

When my Mom and I got to the clinic, Rufus, Geoffrey, Eddie, and Alec were there already, and they weren't having much fun. Personally, I always feel scared of going to the doctor; it's all so white there and it smells of medicine. The rest of the gang had their Moms in tow, too, except for Geoffrey whose Dad is very rich, and he'd come with his Dad's chauffeur who is called Albert. Then Matthew and Max and Jeremy and Cuthbert and their Moms came, and Cuthbert was crying and making a fearful noise. A very nice lady dressed in white asked to see the mothers and collected our vaccination certificates, and she said the doctor would see us soon and please not to be impatient. That was OK, we weren't a bit impatient. Our Moms had started talking to each other and patting our heads and saying what dear little boys we were. Geoffrey's chauffeur went out to polish his big black car.

"You'd never believe the trouble I have, getting my boy to eat," Rufus's Mom was saying. "He's so highly strung!"

"I'm sure they make them work far too hard at school," said Matthew's Mom. "It's ridiculous; my little boy simply can't keep up. In my time …"

"Oh, I don't know about that," said Cuthbert's Mom. "I find my boy can manage the work very well. It all depends on the individual children, you know. Cuthbert, if you don't stop crying, I shall spank you in front of everyone!"

"He may manage the work very well, my dear," said Matthew's Mom, "but the poor child doesn't seem very well balanced, does he?"

Cuthbert's Mom didn't look as if she liked what Matthew's Mom had said, but before she could reply, the lady in white came in and said we could begin getting undressed now, and Cuthbert was sick. Cuthbert's Mom was screeching, and Matthew's Mom was grinning, and the doctor came in.

"What is all this?" asked the doctor. "Really, what a trial these school medicals are! Calm down, now, boys, or I shall get your teachers to punish you. Come on, get undressed!"

We got undressed, and it was very funny being there in front of everyone with nothing on. All the Moms were looking at the other Moms' boys, and they all had expressions on their faces like my Mom's when she's buying fish and she's telling the shop assistant it isn't very fresh.

"Right, children," said the lady in white, "go into the next room and the doctor will examine you."

"I want my Mommy to go with me!" yelled Cuthbert, who was wearing nothing but his glasses.

"All right, all right," said the lady in white to Cuthbert's Mom. "You can go in with him, but do try to calm him down."

"Excuse me, please!" said Matthew's Mom. "If that lady can go in with her son, I don't see why I can't go in with mine!"

"I want Albert to come, too!" shouted Geoffrey.

"You silly nit!" said Eddie.

"Say that again!" said Geoffrey, and Eddie punched his nose.

"Albert!" shouted Geoffrey, and the chauffeur came running in at the same moment as the doctor.

"Oh, really!" said the doctor. "Five minutes ago one of them was sick, and now here's another with a nosebleed! This is getting more like a battlefield than a school clinic!"

"Look here, mister!" said Albert. "I'm responsible for this child, same as I am for the car, and I'd like to deliver them both back to the boss unmarked, OK?"

The doctor looked at Albert, opened his mouth, shut it again and told us (and Cuthbert's Mom) to go into his surgery.

He started by weighing us.

"Come on, you first!" said the doctor, pointing to Alec. Alec asked if he could just finish his little chocolate croissant first, since he didn't have a pocket to put it in. The doctor heaved a sigh, and then he had me get on the scales, and he told Jeremy off for putting a foot on them too to make me seem heavier.

Cuthbert didn't want to be weighed, but his Mom promised him lots of presents, so then Cuthbert got on the scales, trembling like anything, and when it was over he threw himself into his Mom's arms, howling. Rufus and Matthew tried to get weighed together, for a joke, and while the doctor was busy telling them off, Geoffrey kicked Eddie in return for that punch on the nose. The doctor lost his temper and said he'd had quite enough of this, and if we went on acting up he'd give us all some extremely nasty medicine, and he ought to have become a lawyer as his father had advised him. After that, the doctor made us stick our tongues out, and he listened to our chests through a stethoscope thing, and then he made us cough, and he told Alec off because of the crumbs.

Then the doctor got us to sit at a table and gave us paper and pencils and said, "Now, boys, draw whatever comes into your heads. And I warn you, the first one to start any monkeying about will get the thrashing of his life!"

"You just try it! I shall call for Albert!" shouted Geoffrey.

"Go on, start drawing!" shouted the doctor.

So we started drawing. I drew a chocolate cake. Alec drew a steak and French fries with Béarnaise sauce (I wouldn't have recognized it straight off, but

he told me what it was). Cuthbert drew a map of France showing all the regions and the big cities; Eddie and Max both drew a cowboy riding a horse; Geoffrey drew a castle with masses of cars all round it, and wrote "MY HOUSE" underneath; Matthew didn't draw anything at all, because he said he hadn't had advance notice so he didn't have anything prepared. Rufus drew Cuthbert with nothing on and wrote "TEACHER'S PET" underneath. Cuthbert saw it and started crying, and Eddie shouted, "Please, sir, Max is copying!" It was really great, we were having a fabulous time, and talking and shouting, and Cuthbert was crying, and Eddie and Max were fighting, and then the Moms and Albert came in.

When we left, the doctor was sitting at one end of the table, not saying anything, just sighing. The lady in white was bringing him a glass of water and some pills, and the doctor was drawing revolvers.

That doctor is nuts!

Prizegiving Day

The Principal said he saw us leave with deep emotion, an emotion which he was sure we all shared, and he wished us a very pleasant vacation, because once we got back at the beginning of next term, there'd be no more fooling about; hard work, that was what was called for. And that was the end of Prizegiving Day.

It was a fantastic Prizegiving Day. We went to school in the morning along with our Moms and Dads, who had got us up like a lot of proper dandies. We had blue suits and white shirts which were all shiny like the red and green tie Mom bought for Dad, which Dad never wears so as not to get it dirty. Cuthbert, who is nuts, was wearing white gloves, which made us all laugh except Rufus, who said that his Dad, who is a policeman, often wears white gloves, and there's nothing funny about them. And we had our hair plastered down on our heads (I had a cowlick) and clean ears, and our nails were cut. We looked terrific.

We'd been looking forward to Prizegiving Day for ages, me and the gang. Not so much because of the prizes (we were more *worried* about them) but because it would be the holidays after Prizegiving Day. For days and days, at home, I'd been asking Dad if the holidays would soon be here, and did I

really have to go to school up till the very last day, because some people had already gone away and it wasn't fair, and anyway we weren't really doing any actual work at school now, and I was dreadfully tired. And then I cried, and Dad told me to shut up and said I'd drive him crazy.

There were prizes for everyone. Cuthbert, who is top of the class and teacher's pet, got the Arithmetic prize, the History prize, the Geography prize, the Grammar prize, the Handwriting prize, the Science prize, and the Good Behavior prize. Cuthbert is nuts! Eddie, who is very strong and likes to punch his friends' noses, got the Gymnastics prize. Alec, my fat friend who is always eating, got the Regular Attendance prize; that means he goes to school the whole time, and I suppose he really did deserve the prize, because his Mom won't have him in her kitchen, and if he can't be in the kitchen, Alec would rather go to school than anywhere else. Geoffrey, who has a very rich Dad who buys him anything he wants, got the Deportment prize because he's always smartly dressed. There are times when he's come to school in his cowboy outfit or his Martian suit or his musketeer's uniform, looking really great. Rufus got the Art prize because of the big box of colored pencils he had for his birthday. Matthew, who is bottom of the class, got the Good Comradeship prize, and I got the prize for Public Speaking. My Dad was very pleased, though he looked a bit disappointed when our teacher said the prize was awarded more for the quantity than the quality of my work. I'll have to ask Dad what she meant.

Our teacher got prizes, too. We all brought her a present our Moms and Dads had bought. Our teacher got fourteen fountain pens and eight powder compacts. She was ever so pleased, she said she'd never had so many before, not even other years. And then our teacher hugged us all and told us not to forget our holiday tasks, and to be good, and to do as our parents told us, and have a nice rest and send her postcards, and she went off. We all went out of school, and in the street our Moms and Dads started talking to each other. They said a lot of things like, "Well, yours did some good work, didn't he?" and "My boy has had a dreadful amount of illness, you know" and "Our lad is rather lazy, which is a pity, because he has plenty of ability" and "When I was that little rascal's age I was always top of the class, but these days children just don't take any interest in their studies, it's all due to television." And then they hugged us and gave us little pats on the head and wiped their hands because of our brilliantine.

Everyone was looking at Cuthbert, who was carrying loads of prize books and had a wreath of laurels on his head, and the Principal had told him not to rest on them, I expect because the wreath would have to be used again next year and the Principal didn't want it all messed up, like when Mom asks me not to tread on her begonias. Geoffrey's Dad was handing out big cigars to the other Dads, who were keeping them for later, and the Moms were all laughing like mad over the things they were telling each other about what we'd done during the year, which surprised us, because when we actually did those things, our Moms didn't laugh at all, in fact they spanked us.

My friends and I were talking about the super things we were going to do in the holidays, only when Matthew said he was going to save the lives of people in danger of drowning, same as last year, I told him he was a liar, because I've seen Matthew at the swimming pool, he can't even swim properly, and it must be difficult to save someone's life when you can only float on your back. So then Matthew hit me on the head with the book he got for the Good Comradeship prize. That made Rufus laugh, and I thumped Rufus and he started to cry, and he kicked Eddie. Then we all began mucking about. We were having a lot of fun, but the Moms and Dads came and got hold of us and we all went away.

All the way home I was telling myself how great it was, no more school, no more lessons, no more homework, no more detentions, no more fights in break, and now I couldn't see my friends for months and months, and we wouldn't have any chance to play around together, and I was going to be dreadfully sad and lonely.

"Well, you seem very quiet, Nicholas!" said Dad. "It's the holidays at last, you know!"

So then I started to cry, and Dad said this really was too much, and at this rate I would drive him crazy.

René Goscinny

René Goscinny is the world-famous writer and creator, along with Albert Uderzo, of the adventures of Asterix the Gaul. Born in Paris in 1926, Goscinny lived in Buenos Aires and New York. He returned to France in the 1950s where he met Jean-Jacques Sempé and they collaborated on picture strips and then stories about Nicholas, the popular French schoolboy. An internationally successful children's author, who also won awards for his animated cartoons, Goscinny died in 1977.

Jean-Jacques Sempé

Jean-Jacques Sempé is one of the most famous cartoonists and illustrators in the world, whose works are featured in countless magazines and newspapers. Born in Bordeaux, France in 1932, Sempé was expelled from school for bad behavior. He enjoyed a variety of jobs, from traveling toothpaste salesman to summer camp worker, before winning an art prize in 1952. Although Sempé was never trained formally as an artist, more than twenty volumes of his drawings have been published, in thirty countries.

Anthea Bell

Anthea Bell was awarded the Independent Foreign Fiction Prize and the Helen and Kurt Wolff Prize (USA) in 2002 for her translation of W.G. Sebald's Austerlitz. *Her many works of translation from French and German (for which she has received several other awards) include the* Nicholas *books and, with Derek Hockridge, the entire* Asterix the Gaul *saga by René Goscinny and Albert Uderzo.*

Nicholas

Have you read *Nicholas*, where we meet Alec, Cuthbert, Old Spuds, and of course Nicholas himself for the first time?

Nicholas on Vacation

Watch out for *Nicholas on Vacation*. The adventures of Nicholas and his pals continue in this book, the third in the series, coming soon...

To find out more about Nicholas and his friends, visit www.phaidon.com / nicholas